The Pandas Take a Vacation

By Betsy Maestro

Illustrated by Giulio Maestro

A GOLDEN BOOK • NEW YORK

Western Publishing Company, Inc., Racine, Wisconsin 53404

Summer was here. It was time for the Panda family to go on vacation.

"Where shall we go?" asked Momma.

"The mountains," said Poppa. "I want to do some climbing and see some great views."

"I'd like to go to the seashore," said Momma, "so I can find beautiful shells."

Priscilla sat daydreaming. "I want to go on a cruise," she said. "I love boats!"

"And I love wild animals," said her brother Clyde. "A safari would be a real adventure."

Everyone thought about where they wanted to go. But no one could decide on a place they would all enjoy.

Suddenly Priscilla shouted, "Look at this!" She read an ad in the newspaper: " 'Fantastic vacation. Something for everyone. Call Whirlwind Tours.' "

"Let's try it," said Poppa.

"Call right away," said Momma.

Priscilla made the call. "It's all set," she said. "We leave first thing in the morning."

The Pandas spent all day packing.

"Where will we be going?" asked Clyde.

"It's a surprise," answered Priscilla. "We won't know until we get there."

Poppa decided to pack his climbing boots—just in case!

Early the next morning, they all went outside.
After a while, a brightly colored van pulled up.

"Get right in, folks," said a panda in a snappy uniform.
"Let me take your bags."

Soon they were on their way.

"I hope it doesn't take too long to get there," said
Priscilla. "I just can't wait!"

At last the travelers saw a large sign. It said: THIS WAY TO PARADISE PARK. The Pandas had never heard of it. They wondered what it was like.

"I'll bet it has lots of mountains," said Poppa.

"It's probably at the seashore," said Momma.

"It might have a jungle, full of wild animals," said Clyde.

"Maybe Paradise Park is on an island, and we'll have to get there by boat," said Priscilla.

"The ad promised 'something for everyone,'" said Momma. "Let's hope that's really true."

Just then, the Paradise Park entrance came into view.

The van headed down the crowded streets and pulled up in front of the Paradise Park Hotel.

"What a place!" exclaimed Poppa as he climbed out of the van.

The Pandas took an elevator to their room. But before they could unpack, there was a knock at the door.

"Let's go," called their guide. "Whirlwind Tours keeps you moving!"

Outside, the van was waiting. The first stop was a museum. The Pandas wandered through its big rooms, filled with dinosaur skeletons and cases of fossils and rocks.

Soon their guide said, "We're off to the aquarium. We mustn't be late."

Inside the aquarium, fish of all sizes, shapes, and colors were swimming around in large tanks.

Priscilla spotted a shark. "Look at all those teeth!" she cried.

"It's a good thing he's in a tank!" said Clyde.

The Pandas stopped at the gift shop, and then headed back to the van.

After the first day of sightseeing, the Pandas were very tired. Bedtime came, but they were too excited to fall asleep right away.

Priscilla whispered to Clyde, "I can't wait till tomorrow. I wonder where we'll go."

In the morning, the Pandas were off again.

Paradise Park Tower was their first stop. They rode in a huge elevator and climbed some steep stairs. At the top, they could see for miles around.

Poppa pointed to a tiny object far below. "That's our van!"

Next, the van took the Pandas down to the river.
Everyone boarded a sightseeing boat and they cruised far
out on the water. When they were settled, Priscilla set out
by herself to explore the boat.

After a while, Poppa asked, "Where's Priscilla?"

They looked everywhere. Finally they found her with the captain.

"We thought you were lost!" said Clyde.

"Oh, no," Priscilla explained. "I was just helping the captain."

Priscilla and the captain steered the boat to shore, and the Pandas hopped off.

After lunch and an afternoon of shopping for souvenirs, everyone was tired again. At dinner, Momma said, "There's still a lot to see. I'm glad we have a whole week."

"So am I," said Clyde. "I'll have time for a lot more of this fudge cake!"

The week was filled with wonderful places to visit. At the amusement park, the Pandas rode on a merry-go-round...

went into a haunted house...

and took a cable-car ride.

In the Paradise Park Caves, the travelers climbed ladders, slid down chutes, and squeezed through narrow passageways.

On the last day of the trip, the Pandas visited the zoo. They stayed in the van and watched the animals roam around outside. Clyde tried to talk to them, but none of them spoke the Panda language. Clyde was so disappointed!

The day to go home arrived. The Pandas packed up and boarded the van.

"This vacation turned out to be a real surprise," said Poppa. "Each of us got just what we wanted—and a lot more!"

"You're right," said Momma. "We didn't go to the seashore, but I bought shells at the aquarium."

"We didn't go on a real cruise," said Priscilla, "but I went on a terrific boat ride."

"We didn't go on a safari," said Clyde, "but I saw lots of wild animals at the zoo."

"And I climbed the tower and saw my views," said Poppa. "That was just as exciting as the mountains."

The four happy Pandas were so pleased, they sang all the way home.